THE TALE of ALI BABA AND THE FORTY THIEVES

A STORY FROM THE *ARABIAN NIGHTS*

HAPPY
READING!
Will Hillenbrand
2007

RETOLD BY ERIC A. KIMMEL

ILLUSTRATED BY WILL HILLENBRAND

HOLIDAY HOUSE / NEW YORK

In memory of Gus, Squiffin, and Quixote,
Three fine cats.
EAK

For Eric,
One cool cat.
WH

ONCE UPON A TIME two brothers, Qasim and Ali Baba, lived in the city of Baghdad. Qasim, the elder, had shown great skill in buying and selling ever since he was a small boy. He married the only daughter of a wealthy merchant and inherited his property, thus becoming one of the richest men in Baghdad.

Ali Baba, on the other hand, possessed neither talent for trade nor a wife with a fortune. He earned his living as a woodcutter. Every day he led his donkey to the forest beyond the city walls and brought back a load of firewood to sell in the streets. With these meager earnings and his brother's grudging charity, Ali Baba managed to support himself and his family.

ONE DAY, Ali Baba's search for firewood led him to a place in the forest where he had never been. He noticed a dead tree growing out of a rocky hillside. Ali Baba tied his donkey to the trunk. Then he climbed the tree and began breaking off dried twigs and branches. Suddenly he heard the sound of hoofbeats. Looking down, Ali Baba saw a troop of forty horsemen approaching. Each rider carried two leather sacks slung across his saddle.

The riders stopped at the foot of the hill. The *sheikh*, their commander, dismounted. Walking up to a large stone, he pronounced the words:

"Open, Sesame!"

The stone rolled aside, revealing an opening in the base of the hill. The entire band rode in. The stone closed behind them.

Ali Baba trembled, for he recognized these riders as thieves who would kill him at once should they discover his presence. After a while, the stone rolled aside. The forty thieves rode out again, having left their sacks behind. "Close, Sesame!" the sheikh said. The stone rolled over the opening, concealing it as before. Satisfied that their secret was safe, the thieves rode away.

AS SOON AS the band was out of sight, Ali Baba climbed down from the tree. Approaching the stone, he pronounced the words: "Open, Sesame!" The stone rolled aside. Ali Baba walked through the opening.

He found himself in a spacious cavern lit by oil lamps hung from the ceiling. Sacks of gold and silver coins lay in heaps beside piles of rich carpets, silks and brocades, and baskets filled with jewels. Ali Baba dragged three sacks of gold dinars out of the cavern, then said the words, "Close, Sesame!" The stone rolled shut as before. Ali Baba loaded the sacks onto his donkey.

Covering them with firewood to conceal them from curious eyes, he started back toward the city.

Upon arriving home, Ali Baba shut the door and covered the windows. He emptied the three sacks of coins onto the table. There was so much money that the table couldn't hold it all. Gold dinars rained on the floor.

"Father, where did you find such wealth?" Ali Baba's wife and son exclaimed.

"I may not tell you," Ali Baba said, "except to say that I broke no law, nor did I rob any honest man. Come, help me count it."

Ali Baba's wife and son helped him count out their new-found wealth. But with so many coins to count and the hour growing late, Ali Baba decided on a faster way. He sent his son to his brother Qasim's house to borrow the bushel measure.

"What does my brother own that needs to be measured by the bushel?" Qasim wondered. Curious, he smeared a dab of fat on the bottom of the measure. When his nephew returned the measure the next morning, Qasim found a gold dinar stuck to the bottom. He ran at once to Ali Baba's house.

"What is this?" Qasim cried. "Have you become so rich you now measure dinars by the bushel?" He gave Ali Baba no peace until he revealed the secret of the cavern and the treasures it held.

"If one poor donkey can haul away such wealth, think what I can bring back with my twelve strong mules!" Qasim crowed. "Repeat to me again the secret word that opens this cavern."

"'Open, Sesame!'" Ali Baba told him. "And to shut it, you say, 'Close, Sesame!' I beg you, Brother. Do not go. You have wealth enough already. Why risk your life for more?"

But Qasim refused to listen. He led his twelve strong mules to the forest, to the hill his brother described, and tied them outside the cavern. "Open, Sesame!" Qasim said. The stone at the base of the hill rolled away. Qasim entered. The stone closed behind him.

Qasim could not believe his eyes. Here lay more wealth than he ever imagined. He wasted no time in filling his sacks with coins and jewels. As soon as he filled the last sack, he said the words:

"Open..."

Qasim had forgotten the last word of the charm. "It was some kind of seed," he told himself. He frantically tried saying the names of all the seeds he could think of in the hope that one would be right. "Open, Caraway? Open, Barley? Open, Cardamom?"

Before he discovered the correct word, the forty thieves returned. As soon as they saw Qasim's twelve mules,

they knew at once that an intruder had penetrated their secret cavern. They entered and found Qasim. The poor wretch begged for his life. He offered the forty thieves all his wealth if they would spare him. The sheikh refused to listen. He cut off Qasim's head and chopped his body into four pieces. The thieves hung Qasim's remains inside the entrance as a warning to future trespassers.

WHEN QASIM failed to return after three days, Ali Baba went to look for him. Entering the cavern, he found the pieces of his brother's body. Ali Baba wept bitterly as he wrapped Qasim's remains in his cloak and loaded them on one of the twelve mules, which the forty thieves had tethered nearby. He loaded the other eleven mules with sacks of coins and jewels. Then he returned to Baghdad.

HE ARRIVED long after midnight. Ali Baba went at once to Qasim's house, where he summoned Marghana, the slave girl. Unlike Qasim's other servants, Marghana had not been born a slave. She had been stolen from her homeland in Africa, where her father ruled as king. Marghana was beautiful as well as wise, and Ali Baba trusted her as he trusted no one else.

"Trouble rides the first mule," he told Marghana. Marghana lifted a corner of the cloak and beheld her master's mutilated corpse. Ali Baba told her about the hidden cavern and how Qasim had met his end. "I must give my brother an honorable burial," Ali Baba said to Marghana, "but if I bury him like this, chopped to pieces like a common criminal, it will be the talk of the whole city. The forty thieves will surely hear of it. What can I do?"

"Just leave everything to me," Marghana said. Wrapping herself in a heavy veil, she set out for the Street of the Shoemakers. She knocked on the door of a cobbler known as Baba Mustafa. When he opened it, Marghana showed him a gold dinar.

"How would you like to earn this and more for a brief night's work?" Marghana asked him.

"Gladly!" Baba Mustafa exclaimed. A gold dinar was more money than he earned in a month. "What must I do?"

"Three things," Marghana said. "You must let me blindfold you, so you cannot see where I lead you. You must sew whatever I put in front of you without asking questions. And you must not tell a word of this to anyone."

"Agreed!" Baba Mustafa exclaimed. He gathered up his needles, his awl, and his thread. Marghana blindfolded his eyes with a thick bandage. Then they set out through the winding streets of Baghdad, Marghana leading him here and there, until they came to the house of Qasim.

Marghana removed the blindfold. Baba Mustafa beheld a head and a man's quartered body lying before him on a table. Remembering his promise to ask no questions, he proceeded to sew the pieces together with great skill. Marghana paid him two dinars for his work. Then, after blindfolding him once more, she led him back to his house.

The next day it was given out that Qasim the merchant had died after being thrown from his mule while riding in the forest. Qasim received an honorable burial. His wife died of grief two days later. Since they had no children, his brother, Ali Baba, inherited his household and all his wealth.

AS FOR THE FORTY THIEVES, when they returned to the cavern and found Qasim's body, the twelve mules, and two dozen sacks of gold and jewels missing, they realized that someone else knew the secret of "Open, Sesame!" Accordingly, the sheikh sent one of his thieves to Baghdad to discover if anyone had recently acquired great wealth, or died under suspicious circumstances.

The thief arrived in Baghdad late in the evening. As he wandered through the city, he passed a cobbler working by the light of an oil lamp. "I am surprised that you see well enough to sew in such a dim light," the thief remarked.

The cobbler answered, "This is nothing. Why, the other day I sewed up a dead body with a light no brighter than this."

"Indeed?" the thief asked.

"Yes. With the head cut off and the rest chopped into four pieces," the cobbler said, for he was none other than Baba Mustafa.

The thief took a gold dinar from his purse. "This coin is yours if you take me to the house where this occurred."

"Alas, I cannot," Baba Mustafa sighed. "I went there blindfolded and blindfolded I returned."

"Even so, you can still earn the dinar," said the thief. "Allow me to blindfold you, then lead me along as best you remember."

Baba Mustafa agreed. With a blindfold over his eyes, he led the thief the way Marghana had taken him, this way and that, through the winding streets of Baghdad until they arrived at a merchant's house. It was formerly the house of Qasim. Now it belonged to his brother, Ali Baba.

"You have done well," the thief said. He gave Baba Mustafa the promised dinar. At the same time, he marked the door with a bit of chalk.

SOON AFTERWARD, Marghana left the house to go on an errand. She noticed the mark on the door. This aroused her suspicions, but rather than rub it out, she took her own bit of chalk and left similar marks on all the doors along the street.

That night, the thieves entered the city. Their companion led them through the streets along the way Baba Mustafa had shown him. They planned to enter the house with the mark on its door and murder all within. But when they reached the street, they found the same mark on every door, so they had no way of distinguishing one house from another.

After this failure, the sheikh of the forty thieves decided to deal with the matter himself. Taking the disguise of a wandering dervish, he sought out Baba Mustafa and had the old cobbler lead him to the same house where he had led the first thief. The sheikh was much cleverer than his companions. Instead of marking the door, he memorized its appearance so he could recognize it even in the dark.

THE NEXT EVENING, as Ali Baba, his family, and servants sat down to their dinner, they heard a knock at the door. Ali Baba went down to see who it was. He found a man in the stained, dusty robes of an oil merchant standing in the street. A train of twenty mules accompanied him. Each mule carried two oil jars covered with parchment.

"Peace be upon you," the merchant said, bowing. "I am Abul Faraj, a purveyor of fine oils. Is this the house of Qasim the merchant?"

"Peace and Allah's blessing be upon you," Ali Baba replied. "I am sorry to say that my brother Qasim is dead."

"Alas!" the merchant cried. "Your brother promised that if I ever came to Baghdad to sell my oil, I could lodge at his house.

The hour is late. I have come all the way from Mosul. Noble Brother of an Esteemed Friend, could you direct me to lodgings for myself and my mules?"

"Go no farther. You are welcome here as my guest," Ali Baba said.

Of course, Abul Faraj, the oil merchant, was none other than the sheikh of the forty thieves. As to the jars his mules carried, only one contained oil. The rest concealed the members of his band. Abul Faraj led his mules into the courtyard. Before joining Ali Baba at dinner, he went from mule to mule, whispering to the men in the jars. "As soon as the household is asleep, I will throw a handful of pebbles out my window. When you hear them fall, come out of the jars. Make no noise. Have your daggers ready. Remember—no one in the house is to remain alive."

MEANWHILE, unaware of any danger, Ali Baba sent Marghana to tell Abdallah the cook to prepare another meal for their guest.

"Curse my luck! I have run out of cooking oil and the market is closed," Abdallah exclaimed.

"Don't worry," Marghana told him. "Our master's guest is an oil merchant. He has forty jars of cooking oil loaded on mules in the courtyard. Surely, he will not mind if we borrow some." Marghana took the oil jug and the ladle and went down to the courtyard.

As she approached, a voice inside one of the jars suddenly whispered, "Is it time?"

Startled, but keeping her wits about her, Marghana answered, "No. Not yet." She went from jar to jar, receiving the same question and returning the same answer. At once, she realized that terrible danger threatened the entire household.

Marghana filled her jug from the last jar, the one that contained the oil, and returned to the kitchen. She asked for Abdallah's largest kettle. "We have more guests than I expected," she told him. Marghana carried the kettle down to the courtyard and brought it up again, filled with oil. She lifted the heavy kettle onto the stove and set it to boiling.

As soon as the oil began to bubble and seethe, Marghana took the kettle from the stove and carried it down to the courtyard. Swiftly, silently, she moved from jar to jar, pouring scalding oil into each one, bringing death to the thieves before they could cry out.

"One remains, but he is the most dangerous of all," Marghana thought to herself. She needed a plan. Returning to the house, she said to Abdallah, "I wish to dance tonight for our master. Bring your tambor and play for me. I will also need to borrow the old sword you use for chopping vegetables."

"Take it," Abdallah said, "only be careful. The blade is very sharp."

Abdallah went to fetch his drum while Marghana changed into her finest garments. Together they came before Ali Baba. Marghana addressed the household:

"In honor of our guest, and with my master's permission, I would like to perform a sword dance from my own country." As Abdallah beat time on his tambor, Marghana stood before Abul Faraj and began swaying back and forth. Her feet moved faster and faster in time to the drumbeat as she whirled the sharp sword around her head in flashing circles.

Abul Faraj watched, entranced. He grinned at Ali Baba to show his pleasure. Reaching into his purse, he took out a gold dinar and held it out to Marghana. The slave girl danced closer. But instead of grasping the coin, she seized Abul Faraj's wrist and pulled him forward. The sword flashed. In the next instant, Abul Faraj lay dead on the carpet, his head at Ali Baba's feet.

"What have you done?" Ali Baba shrieked at Marghana. "You have slain my guest!"

"He was no guest, but the sheikh of the forty thieves, come to murder us in the night. Your brother Qasim is avenged. Go down to the courtyard. You will find the bodies of the rest of the band in the oil jars."

And so it was.

FROM THAT DAY ON, Ali Baba's wealth knew no bounds, for now that the forty thieves were dead, all the treasures of their cavern belonged to him. Ali Baba gave Marghana her freedom, along with half his wealth, and offered to outfit a caravan to escort her back to her own country. But Marghana had no wish to return to Africa. Her future lay in Baghdad, especially after Ali Baba's son asked her to be his bride.

THUS, through the Grace of Allah,
    Ali Baba the woodcutter and the slave
girl Marghana both achieved wealth and good
    fortune, and so lived happily ever after.

AUTHOR'S NOTE

The Tale of Ali Baba and the Forty Thieves, along with The Story of Aladdin and the Lamp and The Voyages of Sindbad the Sailor, is one of the best-known stories in the collection of Middle Eastern tales known as the Arabian Nights. The episode of the forty thieves may be a reference to the fascinating career of Hasan-i Sabbah, the "Old Man of the Mountains." In the eleventh century this sheikh and his followers established a base in the wild, inaccessible Alamut mountain country, northwest of the site of modern Teheran. The Grand Master of Alamut made his influence felt by dispatching agents to assassinate those who opposed him. Neither sultans nor kings were safe from their daggers.

According to legend, the sheikh plied his agents with promises of heavenly bliss and generous doses of the drug hashish to give them the courage to perform their suicide missions. They referred to themselves as Fida'in—"self-sacrificers." Their opponents called them Hashishin, meaning "those who take hashish." This is the origin of the word "assassin."

The Masters of Alamut maintained their stronghold for over a hundred and fifty years. It was destroyed by the Mongols in 1256.

The art for this book was prepared in watercolor, plaka, and oil pastel on vellum.

Text copyright © 1996 by Eric A. Kimmel
Illustrations copyright © 1996 by Will Hillenbrand
ALL RIGHTS RESERVED
Printed in the United States of America
FIRST EDITION

Library of Congress Cataloging-in-Publication Data
Kimmel, Eric A.
The tale of Ali Baba and the forty thieves: a story from the Arabian Nights /
retold by Eric A. Kimmel; illustrated by Will Hillenbrand. — 1st ed.
p.   cm.
Summary: A poor woodcutter discovers the hidden treasures of a band of robbers,
survives great danger, and brings riches to his whole family.
ISBN 0-8234-1258-X (hardcover: alk. paper)
[1. Fairy tales.   2. Arabs—Folklore.   3. Folklore—Arab countries.]
I. Hillenbrand, Will, ill.   II. Ali Baba.   III. Title.
PZ8.K527Tal   1996   96-33912   CIP   AC
398.22 - dc20
[E]